狄金森诗选

[美] 艾米莉·狄金森 著

王柏华 等 译

(英汉对照)

Selected Poems
Of Emily Dickinson

四川文艺出版社

图书在版编目（CIP）数据

狄金森诗选 /（美）艾米莉·狄金森著；王柏华等译.
—成都：四川文艺出版社，2020.7（2022.4重印）
ISBN 978-7-5411-5158-3

Ⅰ.①狄… Ⅱ.①艾… ②王… Ⅲ.①诗集—美国—近代
Ⅳ.①I712.24

中国版本图书馆CIP数据核字（2020）第065727号

DIJINSEN SHIXUAN
狄金森诗选
（美）艾米莉·狄金森著
王柏华等译

出 品 人	张庆宁
责任编辑	苟婉莹　周　轶
封面设计	叶　茂
内文设计	史小燕
责任校对	段　敏
责任印制	喻　辉

出版发行	四川文艺出版社（成都市槐树街2号）
网　　址	www.scwys.com
电　　话	028-86259287（发行部）　028-86259303（编辑部）
传　　真	028-86259306

邮购地址	成都市槐树街2号四川文艺出版社邮购部　610031
排　　版	四川胜翔数码印务设计有限公司
印　　刷	成都东江印务有限公司
成品尺寸	130mm×185mm　开　本　32开
印　　张	7　字　数　140千
版　　次	2020年7月第一版　印　次　2022年4月第二次印刷
书　　号	ISBN 978-7-5411-5158-3
定　　价	48.00元

版权所有·侵权必究。如有质量问题，请与出版社联系更换。028-86259301

目录

辑一 若是你要秋天来

没人知道这朵小小的玫瑰 -	3
像悲伤一样无迹可寻	5
春日里一点小小的疯狂	9
我品尝从未酿造过的美酒 -	11
知更雀是我评判乐曲的标杆 -	15
有一物在夏日的一天	19
天空低垂 - 层云卑劣	23
把日落用杯子端给我	25
他们唤我到窗前,看	29
若是你要秋天来	33
风的职责很少 -	37
蜜蜂不怕我	41

别以为真如此遥远 43
劈开云雀 — 你会找到音乐 — 45
穿透黑暗的地壤 — 如同教育 — 47
这是鸟儿归来的日子 — 49
控制会持续直至完全得到 — 53
一条渐渐消失的轨迹 55

辑二 云中的罂粟花

愈合的心显示它浅浅的伤痕 59
我的胜利持续到鼓声 61
这是看似平静的一天 — 63
我的生命 — 一杆上膛的枪 — 65
风开始摇动草叶 69
有某种斜光 73
巨大的痛苦后，一种得体的感觉来临 — 77
因为我不能为死亡停下 — 79
颜色 — 等级 — 派别 — 83
他为生命而战 — 87

拒不承认伤口	89
当它们为之歌唱的消散	91
一阵悸痛在春天更显而易觉	93
长年分离 - 没有哪个破裂	95
噢，奢华的时刻	97
通过那传递耐心的事物	99
零度教我们 - 磷光 -	101

辑三 他触摸你的灵魂

可能活着 - 确实活过 -	105
假如最美的时光能够久长 -	107
人性多么钟情于	109
自所有创生的灵魂 -	111
一生能显现于下界的爱	113
"希望"是那种有羽毛的事物 -	117
一种光存在于春天	119
我掂量 - 当我彻底清点 -	123
他触摸你的灵魂	127

说出全部真话，但要曲折地说 -	*129*
他们不知因何事感到孤寂 -	*131*
像双目凝望荒原 -	*133*
我捕捉不到的色调 - 最美 -	*137*
你看我看不到 - 你的人生 -	*141*
她赌上她的羽毛 - 得到一道弧 -	*143*
这桥墩多么易碎	*145*
救助自身更羸弱的部分	*147*
假如我死了	*149*
堆叠如雷鸣直到最后	*153*
那不会妨害她神奇的步履	*155*
以和善的眼睛，回望时间 -	*157*
我总感觉我失去了什么 -	*159*

辑四 岁月流逝后，在黑檀木盒子里

我不愿画 - 一幅画 -	*165*
岁月流逝后，在黑檀木盒子里	*169*
钟停了 -	*173*

又一次 – 他的声音在门口 –	*177*
他们把我禁锢在散文里 –	*181*
我栖居于可能性 –	*183*
我可以跋涉悲伤 –	*185*
我不能证明岁月有（韵）脚 –	*187*
我系好帽子 – 我叠起围巾 –	*189*
我在家里无足轻重 –	*193*
我读信的方式 – 如此这般 –	*197*
阅读吧 – 亲爱的 – 看看别人是怎样奋斗 –	*201*
蜘蛛捧着银色的小球	*203*
诗人唯燃灯 –	*205*
感知一物之代价	*207*
与她晤面后才过三周 –	*209*
我们忙里偷闲的日子	*211*
风敲门 – 像疲倦的男人 –	*213*

◇ 辑一

若是你要秋天来

Nobody knows this little Rose -

Nobody knows this little Rose -
It might a pilgrim be
Did I not take it from the ways
And lift it up to thee.
Only a Bee will miss it -
Only a Butterfly,
Hastening from far journey -
On it's breast to lie -
Only a Bird will wonder -
Only a Breeze will sigh -
Ah Little Rose - how easy
For such as thee to die!

没人知道这朵小小的玫瑰 –

没人知道这朵小小的玫瑰 –
它或许是位朝圣者
倘若我没把它从路边摘下,
呈献于你面前。
只有蜜蜂会把它思念 –
只有蝴蝶,
匆匆从远方赶来 –
在它怀里小憩 –
只有鸟儿才会惊异 –
只有微风才会叹息 –
啊,小小的玫瑰 – 如你这般
多么容易凋零!

(刘守兰译;参考Barbara Mossberg意见)

As imperceptibly as Grief

As imperceptibly as Grief
The Summer lapsed away -
Too imperceptible at last
To seem like Perfidy -

A Quietness distilled
As Twilight long begun,
Or Nature spending with herself
Sequestered Afternoon -

The Dusk drew earlier in -
The Morning foreign shone -
A courteous, yet harrowing Grace,
As Guest that would be gone -

像悲伤一样无迹可寻

像悲伤一样无迹可寻
夏天离我们而去 –
太难以觉察以至最后
不像是背信弃义 –

寂静被蒸馏出来
当薄暮早早就降临,
或是自然在独自消磨着
下午岑寂的光阴 –

清晨显得陌生 –
黄昏提前到来 –
一种有礼却令人痛苦的优雅
犹如客人行将离去 –

And thus, without a Wing

Or service of a Keel

Our Summer made her light escape

Into the Beautiful -

就这样,没有一片翅翼
没有一只舟楫
我们的夏季轻快地逃逸
消失在美的疆域 –

(王晋华、乔亦娟译;参考Gary Stonum意见)

A little Madness in the Spring

A little Madness in the Spring
Is wholesome even for the King,
But God be with the Clown -
Who ponders this tremendous scene -
This whole Experiment of Green -
As if it were his own!

春日里一点小小的疯狂

春日里一点小小的疯狂
甚至也适宜于国王,
愿上帝和小丑同在 –
小丑思量着这壮阔的景致 –
这整个的绿色实验 –
仿佛全属于他自己!

（王晋华、乔亦娟译；参考Gary Stonum意见）

I taste a liquor never brewed -

I taste a liquor never brewed -
From Tankards scooped in Pearl -
Not all the Frankfort Berries
Yield such an Alcohol!

Inebriate of air - am I -
And Debauchee of Dew -
Reeling - thro endless summer days -
From inns of Molten Blue -

When "Landlords" turn the drunken Bee
Out of the Foxglove's door -
When Butterflies - renounce their "drams" -
I shall but drink the more!

我品尝从未酿造过的美酒 –

我品尝从未酿造过的美酒 –
珍珠镂空的酒杯盛着佳酿 –
即使所有法兰克福的浆果
也产不出如此的琼浆!

空气让我 – 如痴如狂 –
在露珠里尽情放浪 –
摇晃着 – 度过无尽夏日时光 –
在迷醉的蓝色酒馆中徜徉 –

当"房东"把那只酩酊的蜜蜂
赶出毛地黄花的门房 –
当蝴蝶 – 放弃他们的"小酒" –
我却要喝到地老天荒!

Till Seraphs swing their snowy Hats -

And Saints - to windows run -

To see the little Tippler

Leaning against the - Sun -

直到天使把雪白的帽子摇晃 –
圣徒们 – 奔往窗户的方向 –
来看我这小醉鬼
斜倚着 – 太阳 –

(王立言译；参考Aaron Dinin意见)

The Robin's my Criterion for Tune -

The Robin's my Criterion for Tune -
Because I grow - where Robins do -
But, were I Cuckoo born -
I'd swear by him -
The ode familiar - rules the Noon -
The Buttercup's, my Whim for Bloom -
Because - we're Orchard sprung -
But, were I Britain born,
I'd Daisies spurn -

None but the Nut - October fit -
Because - through dropping it,
The Seasons flit - I'm taught -
Without the Snow's Tableau
Winter, were lie - to me -
Because I see - New Englandly -

知更雀是我评判乐曲的标杆 –

知更雀是我评判乐曲的标杆 –
因为我与知更雀 – 一起长大 –
但是,假如我生为杜鹃 –
我会以它的名义起誓 –
那熟悉的颂歌 – 响彻正午 –
毛茛花,是我心中花的模样 –
因为 – 我们同在果园绽放 –
但是,假如我生在不列颠,
我会把雏菊踢到一边 –

十月的代表 – 唯有坚果 –
因为 – 经历它的坠落,
四季掠过 – 我知晓 –
没有漫天飞雪的表演
冬天,对我 – 是个谎言 –
因为我以 – 新英格兰的眼光观看 –

The Queen, discerns like me -

Provincially -

女王，眼光跟我一样 –
以家乡的视角考量 –

（王立言译；参考Aaron Dinin意见）

A something in a summer's Day

A something in a summer's Day
As slow her flambeaux burn away
Which solemnizes me.

A something in a summer's noon -
A depth - an Azure - a perfume -
Transcending ecstasy.

And still within a summer's night
A something so transporting bright
I clap my hands to see -

Then vail my too inspecting face
Lest such a subtle - shimmering grace
Flutter too far for me -

The wizard fingers - never rest -
The purple brook within the breast

有一物在夏日的一天

有一物在夏日的一天
她的火炬慢慢燃烬
令我肃然起敬。

有一物在夏日的正午 –
一种深度 – 一种湛蓝 – 一种香气 –
超越心醉神迷。

还有,在夏日的晚上
有一物如此出神地明亮
我拍手凝望 –

然后我遮住我过于审视的脸
唯恐这般微妙 – 闪烁的恩典
会翩然飞远 –

魔术师的手指 – 从不停歇 –
仍有紫色的小溪在胸膛

Still chafes it's narrow bed -

Still rears the East her amber Flag -
Guides still the Sun along the Crag
His Caravan of Red

So looking on - the night - the morn
Conclude the wonder gay -
And I meet, coming thro' the dews
Another summer's Day!

摩挲着它窄窄的床 –

仍有东方擎着她的琥珀旗 –
太阳仍沿着峭壁指引
他红色的篷车远行

就这样守望 – 夜晚 – 清晨
欣欣然为这奇幻的一幕作结 –
穿过露珠,我走来,迎接
夏日的又一天!

(王柏华译;参考Jed Deppman意见)

The Sky is low - the Clouds are mean

The Sky is low - the Clouds are mean.
A Travelling Flake of Snow
Across a Barn or through a Rut
Debates if it will go -

A Narrow Wind complains all Day
How some one treated him
Nature, like Us is sometimes caught
Without her Diadem.

天空低垂 – 层云卑劣

天空低垂 – 层云卑劣。
一片漫游的雪花
争辩它该飞越谷仓
还是穿过车辙 –

狭窄的风整日抱怨
有人待他如此这般
自然如我们,有时被撞见
刚好没戴她的冠冕。

(谢微译;参考王柏华意见)

Bring me the sunset in a cup

Bring me the sunset in a cup,
Reckon the morning's flagons up
And say how many Dew,
Tell me how far the morning leaps -
Tell me what time the weaver sleeps
Who spun the breadth of blue!

Write me how many notes there be
In the new Robin's ecstasy
Among astonished boughs -
How many trips the Tortoise makes -
How many cups the Bee partakes,
The Debauchee of Dews!

Also, who laid the Rainbow's piers,
Also, who leads the docile spheres
By withes of supple blue?
Whose fingersstring the stalactite -

把日落用杯子端给我

把日落用杯子端给我,
测算清晨的酒壶
装着多少露珠,
告诉我,清晨能跳多远 –
告诉我,那织工何时入眠
是它织出了巨幅蔚蓝!

请写信告诉我有多少音符
在新来的知更鸟的迷醉里
在那惊讶的树枝间 –
乌龟究竟跋涉了多远 –
蜜蜂究竟啜饮了多少杯,
那品尝露珠的一族!

是谁,安放了彩虹的基座,
是谁,用柔韧的蓝色柳条
把温顺的星球引导?
是谁的手指串起了钟乳石 –

Who counts the wampum of the night
To see that none is due?

Who built this little Alban House
And shut the windows down so close
My spirit cannot see?
Who'll let me out some gala day
With implements to fly away,
Passing Pomposity?

是谁将夜空的珠贝细数
却发现,没有一颗到期未付?

是谁建造了阿尔班小屋[1]
却又把窗户关得紧紧
让我的精神无法得见?
是谁在欢庆的日子放我出去
让我借装备飞远,
越过凡尘的盛典?

(李丽波译、注;参考Alfred Habegger意见)

---

1 Alban House:隐喻人的肉体,很可能典出圣徒阿尔班的故事。阿尔班是罗马统治英国时期的一名基督教护教者,为了保护一名躲藏在自己家里的基督教牧师,罗马士兵来搜查他的小屋,他穿着牧师的衣服走出来,声称自己就是那名牧师。这里转译为"阿尔班小屋"。

They called me to the Window, for

They called me to the Window, for
"'Twas Sunset" - Some one said -
I only saw a Sapphire Farm -
And just a Single Herd -

Of Opal Cattle - feeding far
Upon so vain a Hill -
As even while I looked - dissolved -
Nor Cattle were - nor - Soil -

But in their Room - a Sea - displayed -
And Ships - of such a size
As Crew of Mountains - could afford -
And Decks - to seat the Skies -

他们唤我到窗前,看

他们唤我到窗前,看
"是夕阳" – 有人说 –
我只见到一个蓝宝石农场 –
和孤零零一群簇 –

猫眼石牛群 – 远处啃食
在缥缈山丘上 –
而甚至当我看时 – 已消散 –
没了牛群 – 没了土壤 –

但那地方 – 一片海 – 显现 –
还有船只 – 这般大小
能容得下一座座山 – 也就是船员 –
以及甲板 – 能让天空上来乘坐 –

This - too - the Showman rubbed away -
And when I looked again -
Nor Farm - nor Opal Herd - was there -
Nor Mediterranean -

这些 – 也 – 被这秀场主持人抹去 –
当我再次注视 –
没了农场 – 没了猫眼石牛群 – 那里 –
也没有地中海 –

（陈义海译；参考Stephanie Farrar意见）

If you were coming in the Fall

If you were coming in the Fall,
I'd brush the Summer by
With half a smile, and half a spurn,
As Housewives do, a Fly.

If I could see you in a year,
I'd wind the months in balls -
And put them each in separate Drawers,
For fear the numbers fuse -

If only Centuries, delayed,
I'd count them on my Hand,
Subtracting, till my fingers dropped
Into Van Dieman's Land.

若是你要秋天来

若是你要秋天来,
我会把夏季扫去
半微笑,半斥责
像主妇般,挥蝇[1]。

若我能在一年内见你,
我会将每月卷成球 –
并将它们分收抽屉里,
避免数字混淆了 –

若只是几世纪的耽搁
我会在掌上算日子,
清数,直到指头掉落
入范迪门之地[2]。

---

1 苍蝇是微不足道的家中常客,在英文中,具有生命力或死亡之引申义,为最后一段的Goblin Bee埋下伏笔。
2 "范迪门之地"是今澳大利亚的塔斯马尼亚省(Tasmania)的旧称,曾是英国流放犯人的监狱。

If certain, when this life was out -
That yours and mine, should be -
I'd toss it yonder, like a Rind,
And take Eternity -

But, now, uncertain of the length
Of this, that is between,
It goads me, like the Goblin Bee -
That will not state - its sting.

若确定，当今生尽头 –
你和我，注定 –
我会抛弃生命，像果皮，
接受永生 –

但，现在，不知等待长短
在此时，与彼时之间，
它驱刺我，像妖蜂般 –
而不显露 – 它的螫刺。

（许立欣译、注；参考Stephanie Farrar意见）

The duties of the Wind are few -

The duties of the Wind are few -
To cast the ships, at Sea,
Establish March, the Floods escort,
And usher Liberty.

The pleasures of the Wind are broad,
To dwell Extent among,
Remain, or wander,
Speculate, or Forests entertain -

The kinsmen of the Wind are Peaks
Azof - the Equinox,
Also with Bird and Asteroid
A bowing intercourse -

风的职责很少 –

风的职责很少 –
让船疾驰,在海上,
创建三月,护送洪水,
给自由导航。

风的乐趣很多,
他的居所无限广阔,
或逗留,或游荡,
或沉思,或跟森林逗乐 –

风的亲属是山巅
亚速海[1] – 昼夜平分点,
还有鸟儿与小行星
和他相互鞠躬,交谈 –

---

1 该词的转喻意义为:波涛、浪花;大洋;大海;湍急的水流。

The limitations of the Wind

Do he exist, or die,

Too wise he seems for Wakelessness,

However, know not I -

风的局限

如果他真的有生死,

他似乎太精明罕有打盹儿的时候,

不过,这一切我并不知道 –

(王晋华、乔亦娟译、注;参考Gary Stonum意见)

The Bee is not afraid of me

The Bee is not afraid of me.
I know the Butterfly -
The pretty people in the Woods
Receive me cordially -

The Brooks laugh louder when I come -
The Breezes madder play;
Wherefore mine eye thy silver mists,
Wherefore, Oh Summer's Day?

蜜蜂不怕我

蜜蜂不怕我。
我认识蝴蝶 –
林子里美丽的人们
热情地把我接受 –

我来的时候小溪笑得更响 –
微风吹得更疯;
为什么,我的眼睛,你会蒙上白雾,
为什么,哦,夏日?

(顾爱玲译;参考杨铁军意见)

Count not that far that can be had

Count not that far that can be had
Though sunset lie between
Nor that adjacent that beside
Is further than the sun.

别以为真如此遥远

别以为真如此遥远
纵有落日横在中间
也别以为毗邻是近旁
它远过太阳。

（周建新译；参考Cindy Mackenzie意见）

Split the Lark - and you'll find the Music -

Split the Lark - and you'll find the Music -
Bulb after Bulb, in Silver rolled -
Scantily dealt to the Summer Morning
Saved for your Ear, when Lutes be old -

Loose the Flood - you shall find it patent -
Gush after Gush, reserved for you -
Scarlet Experiment! Sceptic Thomas!
Now, do you doubt that your Bird was true?

劈开云雀 – 你会找到音乐 –

劈开云雀 – 你会找到音乐 –
一颗颗圆球,流转在银波里 –
几乎舍不得分给夏日的清晨
只为你双耳预留,当鲁特琴老旧 –

松开洪流 – 你会将它尽收眼底 –
一浪推一浪,专属于你 –
猩红的实验!怀疑者多马[1]!
现在,你还怀疑你的鸟儿不真?

(齐悦译;王柏华、齐悦注)

---

[1] 多马,耶稣的十二门徒之一,因其对主的复活采取"非见不信"的态度,被称为"多疑的多马"。据《约翰福音》(John, 20: 24-25):多马怀疑耶稣复活,耶稣让他摸到自己身上的伤痕以证实自己复活。这与"猩红"(Scarlet)一词亦有所呼应。

Through the Dark Sod - as Education -

Through the Dark Sod - as Education -
The Lily passes sure -
Feels her White foot - no trepidation -
Her faith - no fear -

Afterward - in the Meadow -
Swinging her Beryl Bell -
The Mold - life - all forgotten - now -
In Extasy - and Dell -

穿透黑暗的地壤 – 如同教育 –

穿透黑暗的地壤 – 如同教育 –
百合挣出身躯 –
感受她洁白的脚 – 不惊慌 –
她的信念 – 不畏惧 –

然后 – 在牧场 –
摇动她绿宝石的铃铛 –
泥土中的 – 生活 –全都忘却 – 此刻 –
在幽谷中 – 狂喜 –

（冷霜译；参考Leslie McAbee意见）

These are the days when Birds come back -

These are the days when Birds come back -
A very few - a Bird or two -
To take a backward look.

These are the days when skies resume
The old - old sophistries of June -
A blue and gold mistake.

Oh fraud that cannot cheat the Bee.
Almost thy plausibility
Induces my belief,

Till ranks of seeds their witness bear -
And softly thro' the altered air
Hurries a timid leaf.

Oh sacrament of summer days,
Oh Last Communion in the Haze -

这是鸟儿归来的日子 –

这是鸟儿归来的日子 –
很少 – 一只两只 –
回首眷顾。

这是苍穹复原的日子
那古老的 – 六月的伎俩 –
那蔚蓝和金黄的错误。

呵,诡计骗不了蜜蜂。
你的花言巧语
却几乎骗取了我的信任,

直到种子列队作证 –
在微风中轻轻穿行
催促着那一片胆怯的树叶。

哦,夏日的圣礼,
哦,薄雾中最后的圣餐 –

Permit a child to join -

Thy sacred emblems to partake -
Thy consecrated bread to take
And thine immortal wine!

请允许一个孩子的加入 –

烙上神圣的印记 –
品尝神圣的面包
还有你那永生的酒浆!

(刘守兰译;参考Barbara Mossberg意见)

Dominion lasts until obtained -

Dominion lasts until obtained -
Possession just as long -
But these - endowing as they flit
Eternally belong.

How everlasting are the Lips
Known only to the Dew -
These are the Brides of permanence -
Supplanting me and you.

控制会持续直至完全得到 –

控制会持续直至完全得到 –
占有也同样长久 –
但这些 – 他们掠过时所献赠
则永远属其所有。

这些唇会留存多久
唯有露珠知悉 –
它们是永恒的新娘 –
替代了我和你。

（周建新译；参考Cindy Mackenzie意见）

A Route of Evanescence

A Route of Evanescence
With a revolving wheel
A Resonance of Emerald
A Rush of Cochineal,

And every Blossom on the Bush
Adjusts its tumbled Head,
The Mail from Tunis, probably -
An easy Morning's Ride -

一条渐渐消失的轨迹

一条渐渐消失的轨迹
用一个旋转的车轮
一条翠绿的回响
一趟胭脂虫的奔跑,

还有灌木丛中的每一朵鲜花
抬起它耷拉的脑袋,
从突尼斯来的邮件,或许 –
一次早晨轻松的溜达 –

(刘守兰译;参考Barbara Mossberg意见)

◇ 辑二

云中的罂粟花

The healed Heart shows its shallow scar

The healed Heart shows its shallow scar

With confidential moan -

Not mended by Mortality

Are Fabrics truly torn -

To go its convalescent way

So shameless is to see

More genuine were Perfidy

Than such Fidelity.

愈合的心显示它浅浅的伤痕

愈合的心显示它浅浅的伤痕
伴着密不示人的呻吟 –
那已然撕碎的布
岂能缝合,在尘世 –

亮出来,多么不知羞耻,
那伤口已近乎痊愈
背叛反倒是真实可信
跟这样的忠诚相比。

(陈义海译;参考Alfred Habegger意见)

My triumph lasted till the Drums

My triumph lasted till the Drums
Had left the Dead alone
And then I dropped my Victory
And chastened stole along
To where the finished Faces
Conclusion turned on me
And then I hated Glory
And wished myself were They.

What is to be is best descried
When it has also been -
Could Prospect taste of Retrospect
The Tyrannies of Men
Were Tenderer, diviner
The Transitive toward -
A Bayonet's contrition
Is nothing to the Dead -

我的胜利持续到鼓声

我的胜利持续到鼓声
把死者抛在一旁
然后我放下胜利
在自责中悄然回返
到这些亡者面前
这结果将我背叛
于是我开始厌恶荣耀
宁愿我自己是他们。

未来得以清晰地昭示
当它已于当下现身 –
若展望能体尝回顾的感受
人类的暴行
会多些神圣与温和
面对生死交替 –
刺刀的悔过
对逝者毫无意义 –

（许立欣译；参考Stephanie Farrar意见）

It was a quiet seeming Day -

It was a quiet seeming Day -
There was no harm in earth or sky -
Till with the setting sun
There strayed an accidental Red
A Strolling Hue, one would have said
To westward of the Town -

But when the Earth began to jar
And Houses vanished with a roar
And Human Nature hid
We comprehended by the Awe
As those that Dissolution saw
The Poppy in the Cloud -

这是看似平静的一天 –

这是看似平静的一天 –
没有危险,地上或天上 –
直到夕阳沉落的时刻
飘来一朵不经意的红
一种漫步的色调,有人会说
向着城西飘去 –

但当大地开始震动
房屋于巨响中消失
万物生灵藏匿起来
我们才由敬畏领悟
就像那些人见过消融
云中的罂粟花 –

(许立欣译;参考Stephanie Farrar意见)

My Life had stood - a Loaded Gun -

My Life had stood - a Loaded Gun -
In Corners - till a Day
The Owner passed - identified -
And carried Me away -

And now We roam in Sovreign Woods -
And now We hunt the Doe -
And every time I speak for Him -
The Mountains straight reply -

And do I smile, such cordial light
Upon the Valley glow -
It is as a Vesuvian face
Had let its pleasure through -

我的生命 – 一杆上膛的枪 –

我的生命 – 一杆上膛的枪 –
遗立于墙角 – 直至一天
主人[1]路过 – 认出了我 –
并把我带走 –

此刻我们漫游于至尊的树林 –
此刻我们捕猎母鹿 –
每当我代他发话 –
群山立即回应 –

我满脸微笑,明亮温暖
照亮了整个山谷 –
宛如维苏威火山
让喜悦纵情释放 –

---

1 关于"主人",有评论家认为是指诗人心仪的男士,也有人认为是指上帝。我们认为,"主人"指的应该是诗神。

And when at Night - Our good Day done -
I guard My Master's Head -
'Tis better than the Eider-Duck's
Deep Pillow - to have shared -

To foe of His - I'm deadly foe -
None stir the second time -
On whom I lay a Yellow Eye -
Or an emphatic Thumb -

Though I than He - may longer live
He longer must - than I -
For I have but the power to kill,
Without - the power to die -

入夜 – 我们美妙的白昼消逝 –
我守护主人的头 –
胜过把深深下陷的
鸭绒枕头 – 共同分享 –

他的敌人 – 就是我的死敌 –
没有谁能再动弹一下 –
只要我那敏锐的眼睛 –
或是有力的拇指将他瞄准 –

尽管我比他 – 可能活得更长久
他却定会比我不朽 –
因为我只有能力去杀戮,
却没有 – 力量死亡 –

（刘守兰译、注；参考Barbara Mossberg意见）

The Wind begun to rock the Grass

The Wind begun to rock the Grass
With threatening Tunes and low -
He threw a Menace at the Earth -
A Menace at the Sky.

The Leaves unhooked themselves from Trees -
And started all abroad
The Dust did scoop itself like Hands
And throw away the Road.

The Wagons quickened on the Streets
The Thunder hurried slow -
The Lightning showed a Yellow Beak
And then a livid Claw.

The Birds put up the Bars to Nests -
The Cattle Fled to Barns -
Then came one Drop of Giant Rain

风开始摇动草叶

风开始摇动草叶
用低沉、恐吓的曲调 –
他对土地发出威胁 –
对天空发出威胁。

叶子解开树的挂钩 –
到处乱飞
尘土像手把自己掬起
在路上飞扬。

马车在街上加快速度
雷声急匆匆地迟来 –
闪电现出一道黄色鸟喙
然后一只铁青的爪子。

鸟关好巢的门闩 –
牛逃进牲口棚 –
来了一滴巨大的雨

And then as if the Hands

That held the Dams had parted hold
The Waters Wrecked the Sky
But overlooked my Father's House -
Just quartering a Tree -

拦住大坝的手

似乎松开了控制
众水冲垮了天空
却略过了我父亲的房子 –
只把一棵树毁坏 –

(杨铁军译；参考顾爱玲、Jane Eberwein意见)

There's a certain Slant of light

There's a certain Slant of light,
Winter Afternoons -
That oppresses, like the Heft
Of Cathedral Tunes -

Heavenly Hurt, it gives us -
We can find no scar,
But internal difference -
Where the Meanings, are -

None may teach it - Any -
'Tis the Seal Despair -
An imperial affliction
Sent us of the Air -

有某种斜光

有某种斜光，
在冬日午后 –
压抑，犹如大教堂
乐音的重量 –

天国的一击，它给我们 –
伤痕无迹可寻，
但是内里起了变化 –
意义，其所在 –

无人可以揭示 – 些许 –
这是绝望的印戳 –
威严的折磨
在逼人的空气中 –

When it comes, the Landscape listens -
Shadows - hold their breath -
When it goes, 'tis like the Distance
On the look of Death -

当它来临，万物倾听 –
阴影 – 屏住呼吸 –
当它离去，像死亡的一瞥
留下的距离 –

（王家新译；参考Cristanne Miller意见）

After great pain, a formal feeling comes -

After great pain, a formal feeling comes -
The Nerves sit ceremonious, like Tombs -
The stiff Heart questions "was it He, that bore,"
And "Yesterday, or Centuries before"?

The Feet, mechanical, go round -
A Wooden way
Of Ground, or Air, or Ought -
Regardless grown,
A Quartz contentment, like a stone -

This is the Hour of Lead -
Remembered, if outlived,
As Freezing persons, recollect the Snow -
First - Chill - then Stupor - then the letting go -

巨大的痛苦后,一种得体的感觉来临 –

巨大的痛苦后,一种得体的感觉来临 –
神经复归礼仪,像座座坟墓 –
僵硬的心询问"是他,在忍受吗,"
"在昨天,抑或已有隔世之久"?

脚步,机械地,转圈 –
一条木头路
或地上,或空中,或任何什么 –
漠然不顾,
一种石英的满足,像块石头 –

这是铅一般的时刻 –
记住,如果活了过来,
像一个冻僵的人,回想雪 –
首先 – 颤抖 – 然后麻木 – 然后松手 –

(王家新译;参考Cristanne Miller意见)

Because I could not stop for Death -

Because I could not stop for Death -
He kindly stopped for me -
The Carriage held but just Ourselves -
And Immortality.

We slowly drove - He knew no haste
And I had put away
My labor and my leisure too,
For His Civility -

We passed the School, where Children strove
At Recess - in the Ring -
We passed the Fields of Gazing Grain -
We passed the Setting Sun -

Or rather - He passed Us -
The Dews drew quivering and Chill -
For only Gossamer, my Gown -

因为我不能为死亡停下 –

因为我不能为死亡停下 –
他好心地为我停下 –
马车载着,但只有我们自己 –
以及不朽。

我们缓缓行驶 – 他知道无须匆促
而我也放下了
我的劳役和我的闲暇,
为他的礼仪 –

我们经过学校,那里孩童打闹
在课间 – 在一个圆圈里 –
我们经过凝视之谷物的田野 –
我们经过沉落的太阳 –

或不如说 – 是他经过了我们 –
露水让人激颤和冰凉 –
因为我的长袍,犹如游丝 –

My Tippet - only Tulle -

We paused before a House that seemed
A Swelling of the Ground -
The Roof was scarcely visible -
The Cornice - in the Ground -

Since then - 'tis centuries - and yet
Feels shorter than the Day
I first surmised the Horses' Heads
Were toward Eternity -

我的披肩 – 只是薄纱 –

我们停顿在一座房屋前,而它
似乎是大地的肿胀[1] –
房顶依稀可辨 –
屋檐 – 在地底下 –

其后 – 便漫长如世纪 – 但
还是感到短于那一天
我最初猜测这些马头
是朝向永恒 –

（王家新译、注；参考Cristanne Miller意见）

1　Swelling：肿胀、膨胀、隆起。

Color - Caste - Denomination -

Color - Caste - Denomination -
These - are Time's Affair -
Death's diviner Classifying
Does not know they are -

As in sleep - all Hue forgotten -
Tenets - put behind -
Death's large - Democratic fingers
Rub away the Brand -

If Circassian - He is careless -

颜色 – 等级 – 派别 –

颜色 – 等级 – 派别 –
那是 – 时间的事情 –
死神更神圣的区分
不知其中差异 –

如长眠 – 所有色彩遗忘 –
信条 – 抛弃 –
死神巨大的 – 民主的手指
擦去烙印[1] –

即便是切尔克斯人[2] – 他粗心大意 –

---

1 Brand：印记、烙印。例如在奴隶贸易中，奴隶主在奴隶额头或脸部烙烫印记以标明奴隶的身份和归属，这印记将伴随奴隶一生。奴隶或有罪的人在生前因为这些印记、标记而被区别、遭歧视，但当他们死去，死神不予区分，所谓"擦去烙印"。
2 切尔克斯人是一支生活在黑海沿岸、北高加索地区的土著民族，据说是世界上最美丽、最富有色彩的民族。狄金森在此提到他们，一来是暗示即便是色彩如此丰富的人种在死神面前也终将抹去，没有区别；二来是与后文提到的五彩蝴蝶破蛹新生的翩飞相联系。

If He put away

Chrysalis of Blonde - or Umber -

Equal Butterfly -

They emerge from His Obscuring -

What Death - knows so well -

Our minuter intuitions -

Deem unplausible -

错乱收拣
金黄 – 或棕色的蝶蛹 –
都是蝴蝶 –

它们从混沌中破茧而出 –
死神 – 知晓一切 –
我们微小的直觉 –
认为不可思议的东西 –

（曾轶峰译、注；参考Elizabeth Miller意见）

'Twas fighting for his Life he was -

'Twas fighting for his Life he was -
That sort accomplish well -
The Ordnance of Vitality
Is frugal of it's Ball.

It aims once - kills once - conquers once -
There is no second War
In that Campaign inscrutable
Of the Interior.

他为生命而战 –

他为生命而战 –
那一仗打得漂亮 –
生命的大炮
节省弹丸。

一旦瞄准 – 杀戮 – 征服 –
再无第二场战斗
内心的战争
神秘莫测。

（曾轶峰译；参考Elizabeth Miller意见）

A not admitting of the wound

A not admitting of the wound
Until it grew so wide
That all my Life had entered it
And there were troughs beside -

A closing of the simple lid that opened to the sun
Until the tender Carpenter
Perpetual nail it down -

拒不承认伤口

拒不承认伤口
直到它长得那么宽
我的一生都进入其中
旁边还有一条条槽沟 –

向着太阳敞开的那简单的盖子一下阖上
直到那温柔的木匠
永久将它钉上 –

（周琰译；参考Marta Werner意见）

When what they sung for is undone

When what they sung for is undone
Who cares about a Blue Bird's Tune -
Why, Resurrection had to wait
Till they had moved a stone -

As if a Drum went on and on
To captivate the slain -

I dare not write until I hear -
Intro without my Trans -

When what they sung for is undone

当它们为之歌唱的消散

当它们为之歌唱的消散
谁会在意一只青鸟的音调 –
什么？复活必须等待
直到它们已移开了一块石头 –

就好像一面鼓一直敲啊敲
以俘获那被屠杀的 –

我不敢写直到我听见 –
介绍而没有我的翻译 –

当它们为之歌唱的消散

(周琰译；参考Marta Werner意见)

A Pang is more conspicuous in Spring

A Pang is more conspicuous in Spring
In contrast with the things that sing
Not Birds entirely- but Minds -
And Winds - Minute - Effulgencies
When what they sung for is undone
Who cares about a Blue Bird's Tune -
Why, Resurrection had to wait
Till they had moved a Stone -

一阵悸痛在春天更显而易觉

一阵悸痛在春天更显而易觉
对比那些歌唱的事物
不完全都是鸟儿 – 还有心灵 –
和风 – 细微的 – 辉光涌流
当它们为之歌唱的消散
谁会在意一只青鸟的音调 –
什么？复活必须等待
直到它们已移开了一块石头 –

（周琰译；参考Marta Werner意见）

Long Years apart - can make no

Long Years apart - can make no
Breach a second cannot fill -
The absence of the Witch does not
Invalidate the spell -

The embers of a Thousand Years
Uncovered by the Hand
That fondled them when they were Fire
Will gleam and understand

长年分离 – 没有哪个破裂

长年分离 – 没有哪个破裂
不能在一秒内弥合 –
男巫的缺席并不会
让他的魔咒无效 –

千年的灰烬
在还是火的时候
被爱抚它们的手显露
将会闪烁并理解

（周琰译；参考Marta Werner意见）

Oh Sumptuous moment

Oh Sumptuous moment
Slower go
That I may gloat on thee -
'Twill never be the same to starve
Now that I abundance see -
Which was to famish, then or now -
The difference of Day
Ask him unto the Gallows led -
With morning in the sky

噢,奢华的时刻

噢,奢华的时刻
再慢一点去
那样我会为你得意扬扬 -
挨饿将再也不会一模一样
既然我看见富足 -
那时或现在,哪个是去挨饿 -
不同的一日
让他引领走向绞刑架 -
伴同天空的清晨

(周琰译;参考Marta Werner意见)

Through what transports of Patience

Through what transports of Patience

I reached the stolid Bliss

To breathe my Blank without thee

Attest me this and this -

By that bleak Exultation

I won as near as this

Thy privilege of dying

Abbreviate me this

通过那传递耐心的事物

通过那传递耐心的事物
我抵达无动于衷的至福
呼吸没有你的我的空白
向我证明这个,还有这个 –
以那凄凉的欢欣
我如此接近地赢得
你死去的特权
剥夺我这个

(周琰译;参考Marta Werner意见)

The Zeros taught Us - Phosphorus -

The Zeros taught Us - Phosphorus -
We learned to like the Fire
By handling Glaciers - when a Boy -
And Tinder - guessed - by power

Of Opposite - to equal Ought -
Eclipses - Suns - imply -
Paralysis - our Primer dumb
Unto Vitality -

零度教我们 – 磷光 –

零度教我们 – 磷光 –
我们学会爱上火焰
通过触摸冰川 – 当一个男孩 –
和火种 – 猜想的 – 以对方

之力 – 平衡万物 –
日食 – 指示着 – 太阳群 –
瘫痪 – 我们的导火索闷哑
直至获得活力 –

(王家新译;参考Cristanne Miller意见)

◇ 辑三

他触摸你的灵魂

Could live - *did*[1] live -

Could live - *did* live -
Could die - *did* die -
Could smile upon the whole
Through faith in one he met not,
To introduce his soul.

Could go from scene familiar
To an untraversed spot -
Could contemplate the journey
With unpuzzled heart -

Such trust had one among us,
Among us *not* today -
We who saw the launching
Never sailed the Bay!

---

[1] 第一行和第二行的did,以及第十一行的not,狄金森手稿上留有下画线,以示强调,这里采用斜体。

可能活着 – 确实活过 –

可能活着 – 确实活过 –
可能会死 – 确实死了 –
可能正向全体微微一笑
凭着他对未相逢者的信念,
引荐自己的灵魂。

可能正从熟悉的地方
去往未曾涉足的风景 –
可能正用澄明的心
冥想着那段旅程 –

有如此信念的人曾在我们中间,
如今却已不在我们身边 –
我们曾看见船已启航
自己还没有驶离**港湾**[1]!

（罗良功译、注；参考Eliza Richards意见）

---

[1] 原文采用首字母大写形式,这里采用加粗字体,喻指肉身所系之处,"驶离港湾"即指抛弃肉身。

Did Our Best Moment last -

Did Our Best Moment last -
'Twould supersede the Heaven -
A few - and they by Risk - procure -
So this Sort - are not given -

Except as stimulants - in
Cases of Despair -
Or Stupor - The Reserve -
These Heavenly Moments are -

A Grant of the Divine -
That Certain as it Comes -
Withdraws - and leaves the dazzled Soul
In her unfurnished Rooms

假如最美的时光能够久长 –

假如最美的时光能够久长 –
那必将取代天堂 –
极少数 – 冒险 – 获得 –
因此这种 – 就不能给予 –

除非作为烈酒 – 遇到
绝望的瞬间 –
或神志昏迷 – 几许 –
天堂般的时刻 – 就是储备金 –

一种神圣的恩赐 –
会如期而至 –
也会撤回 – 将茫然的灵魂
遗弃在她空空荡荡的房间

(陈义海译；参考Alfred Habegger意见)

How Human Nature dotes

How Human Nature dotes
On what it can't detect -
The moment that a Plot is plumbed
Its meaning is extinct -

Prospective is the friend
Reserved for us to know
When Constancy is clarified
Of Curiosity -

Of subjects that resist
Redoubtablest is this
Where go we -
Go we anywhere
Creation after this?

人性多么钟情于

人性多么钟情于
无法探测的事物 –
一旦定局被探明
其意义就灭绝 –

展望是良友
预留给人们探求
当永恒被厘清
为好奇 –

关于禁忌的话题
这一个最让人畏惧
我们何去何从 –
能去哪儿
在被创造之后?

(许立欣译;参考Stephanie Farrar意见)

Of all the Souls that stand create -

Of all the Souls that stand create -

I have Elected - One -

When Sense from Spirit - files away -

And subterfuge - is done -

When that which is - And that which was -

Apart - intrinsic - stand -

And this brief Tragedy of Flesh -

Is shifted - like a Sand -

When Figures show their royal Front -

And Mists - are carved away,

Behold the Atom - I preferred -

To all the lists of Clay!

自所有创生的灵魂 –

自所有创生的灵魂 –
我选中了 – 一个 –
当精神留下而感觉 – 消损 –
尘世的生命 – 已走过 –
现在的所是 – 与曾经的所是 –
分离 – 内在 – 独立 –
这出肉体的短暂悲剧 –
翻转 – 如沙粒 –
当形体展现其高贵的一面 –
雾霭 – 被剥离,
得见那个原子 – 我独喜它 –
胜过所有的泥坯!

（赖丹婷译；参考Leslie McAbee意见）

The Love a Life can show Below

The Love a Life can show Below
Is but a filament, I know,
Of that diviner thing
That faints upon the face of Noon -
And smites the Tinder in the Sun -
And hinders Gabriel's Wing -

'Tis this - in Music - hints and sways -
And far abroad on Summer days -
Distils uncertain pain -
'Tis this enamors in the East -
And tints the Transit in the West
With harrowing Iodine -

一生能显现于下界的爱

一生能显现于下界的爱
只是一根丝线,我明白,
属于那更神圣之物
隐没于正午的面容 –
在太阳下点燃火绒 –
阻挡加百利[1]的羽翼 –

是它 – 在音乐中 – 暗示和摆动 –
在夏日到达远方 –
萃取未知的苦痛 –
是它迷恋于东方 –
点染变迁于西方
带着苦痛的碘酒[2] –

---

1 加百利:犹太教和基督教传统中的上帝的信使。
2 harrowing:本义是犁地、破土、铲土等,引申为撕裂的、折磨的、摧残的。Iodine:碘酒,一种红色的药水,也指紫红色。首先,作为医用碘酒,它有止痛之效,呼应了诗中的"苦痛"。其次,碘酒的紫红色应和了"点染",渲染了日出和日落的色彩。

'Tis this - invites - appalls - endows -
Flits - glimmers - proves - dissolves -
Returns - suggests - convicts - enchants
Then - flings in Paradise -

是它 – 引诱 – 惊恐 – 赠予 –
掠过 – 微现 – 确证 – 消散 –
重现 – 暗示 – 定罪 – 沉迷
然后 – 抛入天堂 –

（赖丹婷译、注；参考Leslie McAbee意见）

"Hope" is the thing with feathers -

"Hope" is the thing with feathers -
That perches in the soul -
And sings the tune without the words -
And never stops - at all -

And sweetest - in the Gale - is heard -
And sore must be the storm -
That could abash the little Bird
That kept so many warm -

I've heard it in the chilliest land -
And on the strangest Sea -
Yet - never - in Extremity,
It asked a crumb - of me.

"希望"是那种有羽毛的事物 –

"希望"是那种有羽毛的事物 –
它在灵魂里栖居 –
它唱着没有词的歌曲 –
永远 – 也不停息 –

它在狂风中 – 听来 – 最甜蜜 –
这风暴一定很凶猛 –
那样击打这只小鸟
而它却葆有如此多暖意 –

我听过它,在最寒冷的土地 –
和最陌生的海域 –
可是 – 在厄运中 – 它却从未,
索求过我 – 一点一滴。

(冷霜译;参考Leslie McAbee意见)

A Light exists in Spring

A Light exists in Spring
Not present on the Year
At any other period -
When March is scarcely here
A Color stands abroad
On Solitary Fields
That Science cannot overtake
But Human Nature feels

It waits upon the lawn,
It shows the furthest Tree
Upon the furthest Slope you know
It almost speaks to you.

Then as Horizons step
Or Noons report away
Without the Formula of sound
It passes and we stay -

一种光存在于春天

一种光存在于春天
没有出现在一年
任何其他的时段 –
当三月刚刚降临
一抹色彩站立在外
洒在寂寥的田野上
科学无法超越
但人性可以感觉

它在草地上等待,
它投射出最长的树影
在你知道的最远的坡上
它似乎在与你诉说。

然后地平线移步
或是中午报告离开
不拘声音的公式
它离去,我们却停留 –

A quality of loss

Affecting our Content

As Trade had suddenly encroached

Upon the Sacrament -

一种失落的性质

影响我们的惬意

如同贸易[1]突然入侵

一次神圣的仪式 –

（李玲译、注；参考Marilee Lindemann意见）

---

[1] 贸易：南北战争前后，美国经济迅速发展，商贸往来频繁。这对狄金森居住的小镇有不少影响。相似含义的词，如business多次出现在她的诗歌和书信中。

I reckon - When I count at all -

I reckon - When I count at all -
First - Poets - Then the Sun -
Then Summer - Then the Heaven of God -
And then - the List is done -

But, looking back - the First so seems
To Comprehend the Whole -
The Others look a needless Show -
So I write - Poets - All -

Their Summer - lasts a solid Year -
They can afford a Sun
The East - would deem extravagant -
And if the Further Heaven -

我掂量 – 当我彻底清点 –

我掂量 – 当我彻底清点 –
首先 – 诗人 – 其次太阳 –
其次夏天 – 其次上帝的天堂 –
然后 – 名单已经完结 –

但，回头看 – 那第一似乎
就包含了全部 –
其余的已无须罗列 –
因此我写下 – 诗人 – 一切 –

他们的夏天 – 终年持续 –
他们拥有的阳光
东方 – 也会觉得奢侈 –
而倘若更遥远的天堂 –

Be Beautiful as they prepare

For Those who worship Them -

It is too difficult a Grace -

To justify the Dream -

一如他们为其崇拜者
准备的那般美丽 –
就很难证明这梦的 –
恩典确有其实 –

(冷霜译;参考Leslie McAbee意见)

He fumbles at your Soul

He fumbles at your Soul
As Players at the Keys
Before they drop full Music on -
He stuns you by degrees -
Prepares your brittle nature
For the Etherial Blow
By fainter Hammers - further heard -
Then nearer - Then so slow
Your Breath has time to straighten -
Your Brain - to bubble Cool -
Deals - One - imperial - Thunderbolt -
That scalps your naked Soul -

When Winds take Forests in their Paws -
The Universe - is still -

他触摸你的灵魂

他触摸你的灵魂
如同琴师抚弄琴键
在奏响整首乐曲之前 –
他一点一点把你震晕 –
让你脆弱的气质
准备迎接缥缈的锤击
锤子的轻敲声 – 从远处传来 –
然后渐近 – 然后徐缓
你有时间去舒展呼吸 –
你的头脑 – 冒出凉气 –
发出 – 一记 – 庄严的 – 霹雳 –
掀去你赤裸灵魂的表皮 –

当风的爪子抓住树林 –
宇宙 – 一片静寂 –

(刘守兰译；参考Barbara Mossberg意见)

Tell all the truth but tell it slant -

Tell all the truth but tell it slant -

Success in Circuit lies

Too bright for our infirm Delight

The Truth's superb surprise

As Lightning to the Children eased

With explanation kind

The Truth must dazzle gradually

Or every man be blind -

说出全部真话,但要曲折地说 –

说出全部真话,但要曲折地说 –
成功在于回旋婉转
对于我们衰弱的兴奋
真相那辉煌的震惊会过于刺眼
就像被闪电惊吓到的幼童
要用和蔼温柔的解释安抚
应让真理的炫目强光逐渐释放
不然每个人都会变盲 –

(谭大立译;参考Laura Lauth意见)

The lonesome for they know not What -

The lonesome for they know not What -
The Eastern Exiles - be -
Who strayed beyond the Amber line
Some madder Holiday -

And ever since - the purple Moat
They strive to climb - in vain -
As Birds - that tumble from the clouds
Do fumble at the strain -

The Blessed Ether - taught them -
Some Transatlantic Morn -
When Heaven - was too common - to miss -
Too sure - to dote upon!

他们不知因何事感到孤寂 –

他们不知因何事感到孤寂 –
作为东方的放逐者 –
他们越过了琥珀线
在某个疯狂假日 –

此后他们悄悄惶惶想爬
紫色护城河 – 但皆枉然 –
就像鸟儿 – 从云端摔下
摸索回返至力竭而无功 –

神圣的天 – 曾教导他们 –
那个大西洋彼岸的早晨 –
彼时天堂太日常无须思念 –
已握在掌里 – 无须挂心!

（董恒秀译；参考George W. Lytle意见）

Like Eyes that looked on Wastes -

Like Eyes that looked on Wastes -
Incredulous of Ought
But Blank - and steady Wilderness -
Diversified by Night -

Just Infinites of Nought -
As far as it could see -
So looked the face I looked upon -
So looked itself - on Me -

I offered it no Help -
Because the Cause was Mine -
The Misery a Compact
As hopeless - as divine -

像双目凝望荒原 –

像双目凝望荒原 –
难以置信,唯有
空茫 – 无际的蛮荒 –
随黑夜 – 变换 –

不过是空的无限 –
就算目力穷尽 –
我望着的面孔就像这样 –
那面孔对我 – 也像这样 –

我没有给予它任何帮助 –
因为那起因在我自己 –
这苦难,一个契约
既无望 – 又神圣 –

Neither - would be absolved -
Neither would be a Queen
Without the Other - Therefore -
We perish - tho' We reign -

谁 – 都得不到赦免 –
谁都做不了女王
若是没有对方 – 因此 –
虽然我们统治 – 我们消亡 –

(王柏华译；参考Jed Deppman意见)

The Tint I cannot take - is best -

The Tint I cannot take - is best -
The Color too remote
That I could show it in Bazaar -
A Guinea at a sight -

The fine - impalpable Array -
That swaggers on the eye
Like Cleopatra's Company -
Repeated - in the sky -

The Moments of Dominion
That happen on the Soul

我捕捉不到的色调 – 最美 –

我捕捉不到的色调 – 最美 –
那光彩何其邈远
就算我能在巴扎[1]上展示 –
一个基尼[2]只许看一眼 –

那精美 – 不可触知的排列 –
招摇在眼前
宛若克丽奥佩特拉[3]的侍驾 –
于天空 – 重现 –

那主宰的瞬间
临降于灵魂

1　Bazaar（巴扎）一词源自中亚,指大集市,至今仍在中国新疆等地使用,这里取音译"巴扎"以保留其异国情调。
2　Guinea（基尼）为1663年英国发行的一种金币,于19世纪初年停止流通。诗人采用"基尼",除了表示贵重以外,大概也是为了营造某种遥远的距离感。
3　Cleopatra's Company（克丽奥佩特拉的侍驾）很可能典出莎士比亚《安东尼与克丽奥佩特拉》。

And leave it with a Discontent
Too exquisite - to tell -

The eager look - on Landscapes -
As if they just repressed
Some Secret - that was pushing
Like Chariots - in the Vest -

The Pleading of the Summer -
That other Prank - of Snow -
That Cushions Mystery with Tulle,
For fear the Squirrels - know.

Their Graspless manners - mock us -
Until the Cheated Eye
Shuts arrogantly - in the Grave -
Another way - to see -

留下一种怅惘
微妙 – 不可言喻 –

那风景 – 一副热切的神情 –
好像它们刚刚按住了
某个秘密 – 它突突前冲
如战车 – 在背心里 –

那夏日发出的恳求 –
那雪的 – 另一场玩笑 –
以薄纱遮掩神秘,
唯恐松鼠们 – 知晓。

它们不可捉摸的姿态 – 嘲弄我们 –
直到被蒙骗的双眼
傲慢地闭上 – 在墓穴 –
另一种方式 – 去看 –

(王柏华译、注;参考Jed Deppman意见)

You see I cannot see - your lifetime -

You see I cannot see - your lifetime -

I must guess -

How many times it ache for me - today - Confess -

How many times for my far sake

The brave eyes film -

But I guess guessing hurts -

Mine - get so dim!

Too vague - the face -

My own - so patient - covets -

Too far - the strength -

My timidness enfolds -

Haunting the Heart -

Like her translated faces -

Teazing the want -

It - only - can suffice!

你看我看不到 – 你的人生 –

你看我看不到 – 你的人生 –
我须猜测 –
多少次这让我痛苦 – 今天 – 承认 –
多少次为了我的长远着想
那勇敢的双眼迷蒙 –
但我估摸呀猜测令人心伤 –
我的眼 – 已模糊不清！

太模糊了 – 那张脸 –
我一心 – 要看清 –
太难以 – 企及 –
我羞怯颤颤的绵薄之力 –
这萦绕在心 –
如心之多变的脸 –
嘲笑那 –
唯有 – 心可满足的 – 缺失！

（徐翠华、Karen Emmerich译）

She staked Her Feathers - Gained an Arc -

She staked Her Feathers - Gained an Arc -
Debated - Rose again -
This time - beyond the estimate
Of Envy, or of Men -

And now, among Circumference -
Her steady Boat be seen -
At home - among the Billows - As
The Bough where she was born -

她赌上她的羽毛 – 得到一道弧[1] –

她赌上她的羽毛 – 得到一道弧 –
争辩 – 再升起 –
这一次 – 超出
嫉妒,或男人的预估 –

此时,在圆周之间 –
可见她平稳的小船 –
悠游 – 在巨浪之间 – 就像
栖息在树枝,她的出生地 –

(齐悦译;齐悦、王柏华注)

---

1 这里的"弧"首先是一个几何概念,同时还指"向上的轨道""通向天空的道路"。

How brittle are the Piers

How brittle are the Piers
On which our Faith doth tread -
No Bridge below doth totter so -
Yet none hath such a Crowd.

It is as old as God -
Indeed - 'twas built by him -
He sent his Son to test the Plank -
And he pronounced it firm.

这桥墩多么易碎

这桥墩多么易碎
我们的信仰在这桥上踩踏 –
下界之桥不会如此摇晃 –
也没有这般拥挤。

这桥和上帝一样古老 –
其实 – 正由上帝搭造 –
他差遣他的儿子去检验桥面 –
他宣布桥身牢靠。

(陈汐译;参考Eliza Richards意见)

To help our Bleaker Parts

To help our Bleaker Parts
Salubrious Hours are given
Which if they do not fit for Earth -
Drill silently for Heaven -

救助自身更羸弱的部分

救助自身更羸弱的部分
我们有怡人的时光
如若它们不宜活在尘世 –
悄然磨砺它们去往天堂 –

（周建新译；参考Cindy Mackenzie意见）

If I should die

If I should die,

And you should live -

And time sh'd gurgle on -

And morn sh'd beam -

And noon should burn -

As it has usual done -

If Birds should build as early

And Bees as bustling go -

One might depart at option

From enterprise blow!

'Tis sweet to know that stocks will stand

When we with Daisies lie -

That Commerce will continue -

And Trades as briskly fly -

假如我死了

假如我死了,
而你还活着 –
时光仍旧潺潺 –
晨辉[1]熠熠 –
正午灼灼 –
一如既往 –
若鸟儿早早筑巢
蜜蜂闹哄哄出门 –
人们便可以随意地
摆脱下界的事业!
甜蜜啊,得知库存会充足
当我们与雏菊共卧 –
而贸易将继续 –
商业发展飞速 –

---

1 早晨、正午,在狄金森的诗中常具特别含义,而此处当为自然的时辰周转之意。

It makes the parting tranquil
And keeps the soul serene -
That gentlemen so sprightly
Conduct the pleasing scene!

这会使离去[1]时心绪淡定
并使灵魂保持平和 –
当绅士们如此快活地
经营这喜人的一幕!

(周瓒译、注;参考Cristanne Miller意见)

---

[1] 对"离去"时"心绪"和"灵魂"的关注,一方面折射出狄金森写作此诗时的内心动荡,另一方面也体现了她对生命和死亡的态度。

To pile like Thunder to its close

To pile like Thunder to its close
Then crumble grand away
While Everything created hid
This - would be Poetry -

Or Love - the two coeval come -
We both and neither prove -
Experience either and consume -
For None see God and live -

堆叠如雷鸣直到最后

堆叠如雷鸣直到最后
随即轰然坍塌散去
每样事物被创造又被藏起
这 – 可能就是诗 –

或爱情 – 这二者同时来到 –
我们证明二者又一个都证明不了 –
经验其中之一就会毁掉 –
因为没有人看见上帝还能存活[1] –

(周瓒译、注;参考Cristanne Miller意见)

---

1 《圣经·旧约·出埃及记》(35:20):耶和华对摩西说:"你不能看见我的面,因为人见我的面不能存活。"

It will not harm her magic pace

It will not harm her magic pace
That we, so far behind
Her distances propitiate
As Branches touch the Wind

Not hoping for his notice far
But nearer to adore -
'Tis Glory's over-takelessness
That makes our running poor

那不会妨害她神奇的步履

那不会妨害她神奇的步履
我们那么落后
她的疏远给人抚慰
当树枝触摸风

不期冀他遥远的注意
而是更贴近地爱慕 –
这荣耀的不可超越
让我们的奔忙可怜

(周琰译;参考Marta Werner意见)

Look back on Time, with kindly eyes -

Look back on Time, with kindly eyes -
He doubtless did his best -
How softly sinks that trembling sun
In Human Nature's West -

以和善的眼睛,回望时间 –

以和善的眼睛,回望时间 –
他无疑尽了全力 –
那颤动的太阳多么轻柔地沉没
在人的自然的西方 –

(周琰译;参考Marta Werner意见)

A loss of something ever felt I -

A loss of something ever felt I -
The first that I could recollect
Bereft I was - of what I knew not
Too young that any should suspect

A Mourner walked among the children
I notwithstanding went about
As one bemoaning a Dominion
Itself the only Prince cast out -

Elder, Today, A session wiser
And fainter, too, as Wiseness is -
I find Myself still softly searching
For my Delinquent Palaces -

我总感觉我失去了什么 –

我总感觉我失去了什么 –
我被剥夺是我最早的记忆
但被夺走了什么 – 我一无所知
那时我太小不懂得猜疑

尽管如此,在孩童中间
我像个哀悼者走来走去
为失去的领地恸哭不已
是它流放了它唯一的王子 –

如今老了,到了睿智的年龄
可也变得羸弱,因为智者多半如此 –
但我发现我仍温馨地寻找着
我失去的殿宇 –

And a Suspicion, like a Finger

Touches my Forehead now and then

That I am looking oppositely

For the site of the Kingdom of Heaven -

而猜疑，像一根手指
时不时触碰我的额头
于是我朝相反的方向
去把天国的位置寻找 –

（王晋华、乔亦娟译；参考Gary Stonum意见）

◇ 辑四

岁月流逝后，在黑檀木盒子里

I would not paint - a picture -

I would not paint - a picture -
I'd rather be the One
Its bright impossibility
To dwell - delicious - on -
And wonder how the fingers feel
Whose rare - celestial - stir -
Evokes so sweet a torment -
Such sumptuous - Despair -

I would not talk, like Cornets -
I'd rather be the One
Raised softly to the Ceilings -
And out, and easy on -
Through Villages of Ether -
Myself endued Balloon
By but a lip of Metal -

我不愿画 – 一幅画 –

我不愿画 – 一幅画 –
我更愿成为**那一个**[1]
可以 – 悠然 – 栖居于
它那光明的乌有之乡 –
可以想象指尖的感觉
手指轻盈 – 空灵的 – 荡漾
激起如此甜蜜的忧伤 –
如此奢华的 – **绝望** –

我不愿像**短号**一样说话 –
我更愿成为**那一个**
被轻轻地激发,响彻**屋顶** –
再溢出,飘荡开去 –
穿过**天穹**的村庄
我成了丰满的**气球**
经由那**金属**唇片 –

---

1 全诗有十七个词使用了首字母大写形式,译者以加粗字对应。

The pier to my Pontoon -

Nor would I be a Poet -
It's finer - Own the Ear -
Enamored - impotent - content -
The License to revere,
A privilege so awful
What would the Dower be,
Had I the Art to stun myself
With Bolts - of Melody!

我**平底船**的码头 –

我也不愿做**诗人** –
拥有耳朵 – 更好 –
沉醉 – 无为 – 满足 –
那令人敬畏的**特权** –
何等傲人的殊荣
那**嫁妆**将会怎样
假如我能让自己震颤
凭**旋律**的 – 闪电！

（罗良功译、注；参考Eliza Richards意见）

In Ebon Box, when years have flown

In Ebon Box, when years have flown
To reverently peer -
Wiping away the velvet dust
Summers have sprinkled there!

To hold a letter to the light -
Grown Tawny - now - with time -
To con the faded syllables
That quickened us like Wine!

Perhaps a Flower's shrivelled cheek
Among its stores to find -
Plucked far away, some morning -
By gallant - mouldering hand!

A curl, perhaps, from foreheads
Our Constancy forgot -
Perhaps, an antique trinket -

岁月流逝后,在黑檀木盒子里

岁月流逝后,在黑檀木盒子里
用一颗虔敬的心凝视 –
拂去天鹅绒般的尘埃
夏日洒落在那里的印迹!

凑近灯光读信上的字行 –
现已 – 随时光 – 泛黄 –
辨认那模糊的字迹
曾让我们心跳加快如酒浆!

在那黑檀木盒子里或许你会发现
一片花瓣那干瘪的面颊 –
想当初,在远方,某个清晨 –
一只勇敢 – 现已僵硬的手曾将她摘下!

一缕鬈发,或许,来自额头
我们的坚贞曾把它遗忘 –
或许还有,一件古老的首饰 –

In vanished fashions set!

And then to lay them quiet back -
And go about its care -
As if the little Ebon Box
Were none of our affair!

如今早已过时的式样!

默默地,把它们放回去 –
从此不再眷顾 –
就好像这小小的黑檀木盒子
与我们毫无关系!

(李丽波译;参考Alfred Habegger意见)

A Clock stopped -

A Clock stopped -
Not the Mantel's -
Geneva's farthest skill
Cant put the puppet bowing -
That just now dangled still -

An awe came on the Trinket!
The Figures hunched - with pain -
Then quivered out of Decimals -
Into Degreeless noon -

It will not stir for Doctor's -
This Pendulum of snow -
The Shopman importunes it -
While cool - concernless No -

Nods from the Gilded pointers -
Nods from the Seconds slim -

钟停了 –

钟停了 –
不是壁炉架上的那座 –
日内瓦最高妙的技术
也无法让木偶鞠躬 –
此刻它垂悬不动 –

一种敬畏降临这机械！
数字弓背 – 痛苦 –
然后颤抖，从十进制 –
进入无刻度的正午 –

不会为医生动一动 –
这雪的摆锤 –
对于店员的强求 –
是冰冷 – 不关心的否 –

从镀金指针点头 –
从细长秒针点头 –

Decades of Arrogance between -

The Dial life -

And Him -

数十年的傲慢横在 –
刻度的生命 –
和他之间 –

(谢微译；参考王柏华意见)

Again - his voice is at the door -

Again - his voice is at the door -
I feel the old *Degree*[1] -
I hear him ask the servant
For such an one - as me -

I take a *flower* - as I go -
My face to *justify* -
He never *saw* me - in *this life* -
I might *surprise* his eye!

I cross the Hall with *mingled steps* -
I - silent - pass the door -
I look on all this world *contains* -
Just his face - nothing more!

We talk in *careless* - and in toss -

---

1 作者手稿中留有大量下画线,很可能表示强调,这里采用斜字体。

又一次 – 他的声音在门口 –

又一次 – 他的声音在门口 –
我感觉到那古老的高度 –
我听见他向仆人打听
有没有某某人 – 比如我 –

我拿上一朵花 – 走来 –
为我的面孔作证 –
今生 – 他从未见过我 –
我会让他的眼睛吃惊!

我穿过客厅,步履凌乱 –
我 – 无声 – 跨过门槛 –
我张望整个世界的容量 –
唯有他的面孔 – 别无所见!

我们交谈漫不经心 – 而又忐忑 –

A kind of *plummet* strain -
Each - sounding - shyly -
Just - how - deep -
The *other's* one - had been -

We *walk* - I leave my Dog - at home -
A tender - *thoughtful* Moon -
Goes with us - just a little way -
And - then - we are *alone* -

Alone - if Angels are "alone" -
First time they try the *sky*!
Alone - if those "veiled faces" - be -
We *cannot count* -
On High!
I'd give - to live that hour - *again* -
The *purple* - *in my Vein* -
But He must count *the drops* - *himself* -
My price for *every stain*!

一种测深铅锤的拉扯 –
每一下 – 都羞怯地 – 试探 –
对方 – 一直以来 –
到底 – 有 – 多深 –

我们散步 – 把狗留在 – 家里 –
月亮 – 温柔 – 体贴 –
陪我们同行 – 仅仅一小段 –
然后 – 把我们孤单 – 留下 –

孤单 – 如果天使"孤单" –
当他们第一次来到天上！
如果那些"蒙着面纱的脸" – 如此 –
我们不能指望 –
高高在上！
我愿献出我血管里的 – 紫红 –
为了 – 重返那个时刻 – 再一次 –
但他必须亲自 – 细数 –
我的代价每一滴！

（王柏华译、注；参考Julie Enszer意见）

They shut me up in Prose -

They shut me up in Prose -
As when a little Girl
They put me in the Closet -
Because they liked me "still" -

Still! Could themself have peeped -
And see my Brain - go round -
They might as wise have lodged a Bird
For Treason - in the Pound -

Himself has but to will
And easy as a Star
Look down upon Captivity -
And laugh - No more have I -

他们把我禁锢在散文里 –

他们把我禁锢在散文里 –
当我还是女孩儿时
他们把我关进壁柜里 –
想让我"闭嘴不动" –

闭嘴不动!如果他们能够 –
偷窥我的大脑 – 它在转动 –
明智如他们,居然以反叛罪名
控诉小鸟 – 关他入狱 –

他自己只需轻而易举
就能像星星那样
轻蔑地俯视这囚禁 –
开怀而笑 – 我再也没有 –

(谭大立译;参考Laura Lauth意见)

I dwell in Possibility -

I dwell in Possibility -
A fairer House than Prose -
More numerous of Windows -
Superior - for Doors -

Of Chambers as the Cedars -
Impregnable of eye -
And for an everlasting Roof
The Gambrels of the Sky -

Of Visitors - the fairest -
For Occupation - This -
The spreading wide my narrow Hands
To gather Paradise -

我栖居于可能性 –

我栖居于可能性 –
一座比散文更美的房子 –
窗户 – 更多更亮 –
房门 – 都很雄壮 –

雪松般的厅堂 –
双眼看不到天花板 –
它那永恒的屋顶
苍穹般的三角墙 –

来客们 – 都是完美的人 –
这就是 – 我的职业 –
伸展我狭小的双手
采集天堂乐园 –

　　　　　　　　（谭大立译；参考Laura Lauth意见）

I can wade Grief -

I can wade Grief -
Whole Pools of it -
I'm used to that -
But the least push of Joy
Breaks up my feet -
And I tip - drunken -
Let no Pebble - smile -
'Twas the New Liquor -
That was all!

Power is only Pain -
Stranded - thro' Discipline,
Till Weights - will hang -
Give Balm - to Giants -
And they'll wilt, like Men -
Give Himmaleh -
They'll carry - Him!

我可以跋涉悲伤 –

我可以跋涉悲伤 –
整池整池地走过 –
我早已处之泰然 –
不过喜悦仅轻轻一推
我就摔跤 –
我因喝醉而绊倒 –
小石子可别取笑 –
是新酒惹的祸 –
就这么回事!

力量不过是痛苦 –
经受磨炼出来的,
直到可以 – 负荷重担 –
给巨人 – 抚慰 –
他们会变脆弱,像凡人 –
给喜马拉雅山 –
他们就举起 – 他!

(董恒秀译;参考George W. Lytle意见)

I could not prove the Years had feet -

I could not prove the Years had feet -
Yet confident they run
Am I, from symptoms that are past
And Series that are done -

I find my feet have further Goals -
I smile upon the Aims
That felt so ample - Yesterday -
Today's - have vaster claims -

I do not doubt the Self I was
Was competent to me -
But something awkward in the fit -
Proves that - outgrown - I see -

我不能证明岁月有(韵)脚 –

我不能证明岁月有(韵)脚[1] –
但我确信它们在奔跑
从那往日的痕迹
和那完成的系列 –

我发现脚下有更远的目标 –
含笑面对以往之目的地
曾经是那么充实 – 昨日 –
今日 – 拥有更宏大的领地 –

我不怀疑过去的我
合适而能胜任 –
可是不自在的"小号" –
已证明 – 我长了 – 我看到 –

(谭大立译、注;参考Laura Lauth意见)

---

[1] feet:一语双关,既是脚(身体部位),也是诗歌的韵律,这里采用(韵)脚来体现这一双关。

I tie my Hat - I crease my Shawl -

I tie my Hat - I crease my Shawl -
Life's little duties do - precisely -
As the very least
Were infinite - to me -

I put new Blossoms in the Glass -
And throw the Old - away -
I push a petal from my Gown
That anchored there - I weigh
The time 'twill be till six o'clock -
So much I have to do -
And yet - existence - some way back -
Stopped - struck - my ticking - through -

We cannot put Ourself away
As a completed Man
Or Woman - When the errand's done
We came to Flesh - upon -

我系好帽子 – 我叠起围巾 –

我系好帽子 – 我叠起围巾 –
生活的小小义务 – 一丝不苟地履行 –
好像琐细之至
对于我 – 却是无限终极 –

我把鲜花放入玻璃瓶 –
把旧的 – 丢出去 –
我拂去一片花瓣从我的外袍
它之前在那里停靠 – 我掂量着
时间,直到六点之前 –
多少事我必须做好 –
可是 – 存在 – 不久前 –
既已停摆 – 我的嘀嗒 – 已敲完 –

我们无法把自己丢开了事
像一个完结的男人
或女人 – 当使命已结束
我们曾为此 – 化为肉身 –

There may be - Miles on Miles of Nought -

Of Action - sicker far -

To simulate - is stinging work -

To cover what we are

From Science - and from Surgery -

Too Telescopic eyes

To bear on us unshaded -

For their - sake - Not for Ours -

Therefore - we do life's labor -

Though life's Reward - be done -

With scrupulous exactness -

To hold our Senses - on -

或许前方－是虚空一里又一里－
是动作－何其倦怠无力－
伪装－是一种煎熬－
试图把我们的真相藏起

躲开科学－躲开外科－
那望远镜式的窥探
瞄准我们毫不遮蔽－
不是为我们－而是为它们自己－

因此－我们为生活做工－
虽然生命的奖赏－既已成空－
以小心翼翼的精确－
将我们的理智－支撑－

（王柏华译；参考Jed Deppman意见）

I was the slightest in the House -

I was the slightest in the House -
I took the smallest Room -
At night, my little Lamp, and Book -
And one Geranium -

So stationed I could catch the mint
That never ceased to fall -
And just my Basket -
Let me think - I'm sure -
That this was all -

I never spoke - unless addressed -
And then, 'twas brief and low -
I could not bear to live - aloud -
The Racket shamed me so -

我在家里无足轻重 –

我在家里无足轻重 –
我住最小的房间 –
晚上,小台灯,和书 –
还有天竺葵相伴 –

这样住着我能接到财富[1]
它从不停止下落 –
只有我的筐篓 –
让我思索 – 我确信 –
这是全部 –

我从不讲话 – 除非有人搭讪 –
而我的应答,低沉且简短 –
我难以忍受 – 喧嚷的生活 –
喧闹让我深感丢脸 –

---

[1] mint:铸币厂、巨额、薄荷属植物、薄荷糖、有价值的东西等。第一小节诗人在读书,因此,此处的mint或可理解为巨额精神财富或者令人感到耳目一新的思想或灵感。

And if it had not been so far -
And any one I knew
Were going - I had often thought
How noteless - I could die -

要不是天堂太遥远 –
要不是有熟人
即将前往 – 我常想
我会死得 – 多么寂寂无名 –

（王立言译、注；参考Aaron Dinin意见）

The Way I read a Letter's - this -

The Way I read a Letter's - this -
'Tis first - I lock the Door -
And push it with my fingers - next -
For transport it be sure -

And then I go the furthest off
To counteract a knock -
Then draw my little Letter forth
And slowly pick the lock -

Then - glancing narrow, at the Wall -
And narrow at the floor
For firm Conviction of a Mouse
Not exorcised before -

我读信的方式 – 如此这般 –

我读信的方式 – 如此这般 –
首先 – 我把门儿锁上 –
接着 – 用手指轻推试探 –
确保读得心驰神往 –

之后我走到房间的远角
想抵抗敲门声的干扰 –
尔后拿出我小小的信
并慢慢地拆开封条 –

然后 – 眯着眼,看看墙壁 –
再眯眼看看地面
确保没有一只耗子
以前未被赶跑 –

Peruse how infinite I am

To no one that You - know -

And sigh for lack of Heaven - but not

The Heaven God bestow -

读出我的莫逆之契
写信人 – 你无从晓畅 –
嗟叹没有天堂 – 但不嗟叹
没有上帝赐予的天堂 –

(王立言译；参考Aaron Dinin意见)

Read - Sweet - how others - strove -

Read - Sweet - how others - strove -
Till we - are stouter -
What they - renounced -
Till we - are less afraid -
How many times they - bore the faithful witness -
Till we - are helped -
As if a Kingdom - cared!

Read then - of faith -
That shone above the fagot -
Clear strains of Hymn
The River could not drown -
Brave names of Men -
And Celestial Women -
Passed out - of Record
Into - Renown!

阅读吧 – 亲爱的 – 看看别人是怎样奋斗 –

阅读吧 – 亲爱的 – 看看别人是怎样奋斗 –
直到我们 – 也更加坚强 –
看看他们 – 放弃了什么 –
直到我们 – 也不再那么害怕 –
看看多少次 – 他们忠于自己的观察 –
直到我们 – 也从中获益 –
好比一个王国 – 小心翼翼!

再读读 – 信念 –
经历血与火考验的信念 –
读读那滔滔江水
也无法掩去的悦耳的音乐 –
读读那些勇敢的男人 –
和非凡的女人的名 –
看他们怎样超越 – 平庸
而 – 出人头地!

(徐翠华、Karen Emmerich译)

The Spider holds a Silver Ball

The Spider holds a Silver Ball
In unperceived Hands -
And dancing softly to Himself
His Yarn of Pearl - unwinds -

He plies from Nought to nought -
In unsubstantial Trade -
Supplants our Tapestries with His -
In half the period -

An Hour to rear supreme
His Continents of Light -
Then dangle from the Housewife's Broom -
His Boundaries - forgot -

蜘蛛捧着银色的小球

蜘蛛捧着银色的小球
用无形的手 –
他轻轻起舞,独自一人
珍珠纱线 – 徐徐展开 –

从无到无 –
他经营着无足轻重的事业 –
将我们的织锦换成他的 –
只需前半段 –

一小时就升起至高之物
他的光之大陆 –
随后便飘摇在主妇的
笤帚之下 –
他的边界 – 已然遗忘 –

(陈汐译;参考Eliza Richards意见)

The Poets light but Lamps -

The Poets light but Lamps -
Themselves - go out -
The Wicks they stimulate
If vital Light

Inhere as do the Suns -
Each Age a Lens -
Disseminating their -
Circumference -

诗人唯燃灯 –

诗人唯燃灯 –
他们自己 – 走开 –
捻亮灯蕊
设若**光**常在

蓬勃如朗朗**众**日 –
每**纪元**一**透镜** –
播散自身之 –
圆[1] –

(杨炼译、注;参考Eliza Richards意见)

---

1 Circumference:按照狄金森的词典,这个词的含义极其丰富,既可以指圆的形状、圆形的区域,也可以指事物的边界、看问题的角度,甚至是永恒的真理,这和上文将"世纪"比作"透镜"有一致之处。译文取"圆周""边界"这一较为基本的含义。

Perception of an Object costs

Perception of an Object costs
Precise the Object's loss -
Perception in itself a Gain
Replying to its Price -

The Object absolute, is nought -
Perception sets it fair
And then upbraids a Perfectness
That situates so far -

感知一物之代价

感知一物之代价
恰合**物**之耗损 –
感知增益自身
回应物之消殒 –

此**物**全然,是无 –
感知还其均衡
稍后却责备**完美**
如此迢遥 –

　　　　　　　(杨炼译;参考Eliza Richards意见)

Three Weeks passed since I had seen Her -

Three Weeks passed since I had seen Her -
Some Disease had vext
'Twas with Text and Village Singing
I beheld Her next

And a Company - our pleasure
To discourse alone -
Gracious now to me as any -
Gracious unto none -

Borne without dissent of Either
To the Parish night -
Of the Separated Parties
Which be out of sight?

与她晤面后才过三周 –

与她晤面后才过三周 –
某种疾病已发难
透过文告和村庄的吟唱
我与她再次相见

还有众人 – 我们曾愉快
促膝交谈 –
如今感觉亲切无比 –
但无人有同感 –

双方均无异议
承受着这教区的夜晚 –
在散去的人群里
有谁已经消逝?

(周建新译;参考Cindy Mackenzie意见)

The Days that we can spare

The Days that we can spare
Are those a Function die
Or Friend Or Nature - stranded then
In our Economy

Our Estimates a Scheme -
Our Ultimates a Sham -
We let go all of Time without
Arithmetic of him -

我们忙里偷闲的日子

我们忙里偷闲的日子
唯在某项功能丧失
或是朋友或大自然 – 困顿之时
因我们如此吝惜

我们的憧憬仅是一个计划 –
我们的目标无异于一个骗局 –
我们放逐全部光阴
从未——算计 –

(周建新译;参考Cindy Mackenzie意见)

The Wind - tapped like a tired Man -

The Wind - tapped like a tired Man -
And like a Host - "Come in"
I boldly answered - entered then
My Residence within

A Rapid - footless Guest -
To offer whom a Chair
Were as impossible as hand
A Sofa to the Air -

No Bone had He to bind Him -
His Speech was like the Push
Of numerous Humming Birds at once
From a superior Bush -

His Countenance - a Billow -
His Fingers, as He passed
Let go a music - as of tunes

风敲门 – 像疲倦的男人 –

风敲门 – 像疲倦的男人 –
像主人一样 – "请进"
我大胆回应 – 然后
我的访客进了门

飞快的 – 没脚的客人 –
给他一把椅子坐
就像把沙发递给空气
同样是不可能的 –

他的身体没有骨头支撑 –
他的话语像蜂鸟
从一棵高高的灌木
一瞬间飞出一大群 –

他的表情 – 海浪 –
手指,当他一闪而过
发出 – 微颤的曲调

Blown tremulous in Glass -

He visited - still flitting -
Then like a timid Man
Again, He tapped - 'twas flurriedly -
And I became alone -

好像吹自一块玻璃 –

他来拜访 – 仍是摇摆不定 –
然后,像个男人怯生生
再次敲门 – 忽忽的 –
我变得孤单一人 –

(顾爱玲译;参考杨铁军意见)